RAINBOW
LAUGHTER

ALSO BY VERONICA BRIGHT

SHORT STORY COLLECTIONS

Cloud Paintings

A Gift from the Horse Chestnut Tree

NON-FICTION

Frogs in Assembly:
Plays for Children in Key Stage One
Published by Kevin Mayhew

Robots in Assembly:
Plays for Children in Key Stage One
Published by Kevin Mayhew

RAINBOW LAUGHTER

A collection of prize-winning stories

Veronica Bright

Published in Great Britain, 2017

All rights reserved

This is a work of fiction. The characters and events described herein are imaginary and are not intended to refer to specific places or to persons alive or dead. No part of this publication may be reproduced, stored in a retrieval system, distributed, or transmitted in any form or by any means, including photocopying, recording, or other electronic or mechanical methods, without the prior written permission of the copyright owners, except for brief quotations embodied in critical reviews. Nor can it be circulated in any form of binding or cover other than that in which it is published and without similar condition including this condition being imposed upon a subsequent purchaser.

ISBN: 978-1548446567

© Veronica Bright 2017

Cover photo: East Looe, Cornwall, by Chris Roper

For my family

with love

CONTENTS

Feeding the Birds	1
The Next Instalment	7
The Whole-Face Smile	20
The Sign	26
Stargazing	37
A Bit of Peace and Quiet	45
Mr Wacker's Quay	55
The Last Rays	64
Rainbow Laughter	70
About the Stories	79
About the Author	81

Feeding the Birds

The leaves scutter and drift. I pull my faithful old coat round me, adjust my headscarf. The Queen wears these, against the wind. Better quality than this I expect, but you never know. I found it in the charity shop next to the ironmonger's. Before he closed for good.

I watch the children going to school, laughing or tearful. Same faces every day. One's called Molly. Pretty name, Molly. Always dancing she is. They live in my block, but I don't suppose they know we're neighbours. I lead a quiet life now.

Another child's called Davy. He was ill last winter. Pneumonia. I heard his mother talking to a friend as she went by. She always has a worried frown; makes him walk beside her and hold her hand. Same time every morning, except weekends of course. I think I mutter sometimes, lines of old plays that seem just right for the moment, that kind of thing. Probably unsettles the woman. But who else have I got to talk to these days? Elizabeth's gone, and Margo doesn't know what day of the week it is. And Henry's in that home in Southend, near his daughter.

The teenage boys come by, their ties short. They kick the leaves, the odd stone. They push each other. They laugh, their deep voices carrying them into manhood. The girls are different. They chatter and giggle. Short skirts, trousers some of them. The world at their feet.

I reach into the old brown bag – I've had it for years, it's like a friend – and I rummage for the bread. I take out a chunk of crust, holding it with shaky fingers, crumbling it into tiny beak-size pieces. The pigeons arrive first, then the sparrows; a couple of chaffinches; sometimes a thrush if I'm lucky.

Today a seagull lands with a soft thud on the grass, tries to look natural, sizes up the situation. Then he's in the middle of the crowd, a bit of a bully, snatching the biggest bits, ducking and diving. The chaffinches flutter upwards, showing small flashes of white, a black streak in their tails. The sparrows dart.

'Hey Missis, you shouldn't feed the seagulls.'

It's the sturdy little chap from the next block of flats. I ignore his remark, and look at the leaves on the beech tree. They're turning that beautiful russet brown I used to wear when my hair was almost the same shade.

I've grown used to anonymity. I can walk the whole length of the high street and remain invisible. I shuffle my scarf into a better position. I blink at the child in front of me.

'Harry, I've told you.' Harry's mother is a woman who obviously likes her dinners. She's panting with the effort of keeping up. 'You are not to talk to strangers. Ever.'

'But...'

'End of story.'

She gives him a small push and puffs off, waddling slightly. Harry lingers for a moment, then he's away at a gallop, riding an imaginary horse.

'Who is that, Mum?' he shouts at her.

'Nobody important,' she replies.

Nobody important. A stranger. Am I really a stranger? I'm here every morning, well, most mornings, though last winter's ice did stop me for a while. The days when it's raining cats and dogs. My eyes follow the children, my ears catch their tears or their laughter. My thoughts strain back down the years.

Nobody important.

'Melanie!'

I was somebody once.

'You are, aren't you? Melanie Harper?'

There's a gent in front of me.

'Sorry if I'm wrong.'

Harry's mother's warning about not talking to strangers floats around in my head.

'You know me!'

Arms spread wide.

'Bill Knightfield. Brighton 1956. Torquay 62. Remember now?'

The man sits uninvited beside me. He's wearing a smart brown coat and a dapper little hat. Suddenly he begins to recount the story of my life.

'You were always the best, gal,' he says. 'Remember that Fred and Ginger number we did together?'

'Bill,' I say, in a voice which may be questioning who on earth he is, or on the other hand, may be confirming in shock that I remember him well.

'Melanie! Come on. Let's have a coffee for old times' sake.'

As I carefully tip the rest of the crumbs onto the ground, I notice Bill's polished shoes. I shift my aching bunions inside my shabby boots.

'Melanie Harper. Remember that first night in Swansea? Remember the headline? "A talented new star," that reporter wrote. "This young lady is charm personified."'

All hidden now, I think, hidden beneath comfortable clothes – hardly à la mode any more – and under this old suitcase of a body, battered and worn and needing to be put firmly somewhere out of sight. I sigh. And when I look up there is just the street-cleaner with his paper-grabber. He's staring at me, and I know I've been day-dreaming again. Muttering too probably.

'I am old,' I say quietly, as if that will explain everything.

He's probably never noticed me before, though I always say good morning. His hand rests on the handle of his small cart, and he's stopped prodding carefully at the rubbish, clearing away the debris of life with a certain pride.

'Everything I have been, has gone,' I whisper. I look up at the street-cleaner's face.

'Take no notice,' I say, 'I am nobody important.'

'That's where you're wrong,' says the street-cleaner. And he smiles at me, a perfect, friendly, kindly smile.

And from the far distant past, when I was young and pretty and really quite famous, a voice tells me to shrug off this feeling of being old and useless, fit for nothing more than feeding the birds in the park, so I smile back.

'Thank you,' I say.

As I stand up the sun breaks through. The leaves scutter and drift. I smooth my faithful old coat. Then I take off my headscarf, shake free my rather wispy hair, and step out firmly along the path.

The Next Instalment

'No buts, remember?'

'I didn't want to. I would never... Wait, I... Wait.'

Lauren's mobile is dead. Her face is the colour of putty. There is a faint whine from the ground. Sproggs gazes at her as if she has deliberately hidden his bone. Lauren tugs the lead, and he waddles on.

Back at the big house, Mrs Lavender limps to the kitchen

'Lemonade?' she asks, as Lauren follows her. She turns, then stops. 'What's the matter, dear?'

Lauren hesitates. Mrs Lavender has been very kind to her ever since she answered the dog-walking advertisement in the newsagent's.

That was a year ago, and since then she's nervously asked Mrs Lavender if she could please do some other jobs for her, too. She needed to earn some money, she said, quite a lot of money, in fact. Everyone knows her mum is, well, not in the best of health. Some people call her a dosser, or worse. They cross the street when they see her coming. But Lauren knows it isn't easy to bring up three children on your own, especially when you have 'a terrible weakness,' as her mother says. For years Lauren thought this was some kind of medical condition. Which it is really.

'I want to go to France,' she said. 'With the school.'

'And your mother can't afford it.'

It wasn't a question.

'I'm willing to work hard. I'm honest.' Lauren looked Mrs Lavender in the eye. 'I tell the truth.'

'Do you know anything about gardening?'

'I can learn.'

Now, weeks later, Lauren is shifting from foot to foot in Mrs Lavender's kitchen.

'So, what's the trouble?' she is asking, 'Has Sproggs been playing you up?'

Lauren shakes her head.

'It's just some-one at school... spreading lies about me.'

'Oh my dear. You must try hard to ignore those unkind words.'

Lauren bites her lip and turns to pat the dog's solemn head.

Mrs Lavender finds her purse. 'Thank you for looking after Sproggs. And don't worry. Just remember what I said. Ignore.'

Lauren runs all the way home.

'That you, Lauren?'

'Yes, Mum.'

'Make the tea for us, duck. I'm having a bit of a lie-down.'

Lauren checks the living room. Little Amber doesn't look up from the television. There's no sign of Spencer, but he'll be back soon enough. When he's hungry.

Lauren stands by the sink and starts peeling potatoes. If Kerry doesn't want to listen to her explanation, who will? Well, whatever anyone says, it's not stealing. She's going to put it back. She had to do it, didn't she? It was the deadline for the £40 instalment, and she wanted to go to France so much. She'd been thinking about it for weeks; staying with a real French family, then later on her 'correspondent' would come and stay with her. Lauren is a bit stressed about that. She doesn't think they know at school. About her mum and her problem. But Mum's OK. She loves them all, doesn't she? She often cries and says she isn't any good for them, and then they say yes she is, she's their mum. She just has a weakness, that's all.

Lauren had worried about Spencer and Amber coping while she's away, too, but Mrs Lavender said she'd find someone to look after things.

Lauren remembers the day she took her deposit to school. Excitement had fluttered in her stomach. She'd wanted to hang a French flag from her bedroom window and sing the Marseillaise.

Now, preparing potatoes, the thing Lauren's stomach feels is fear. A tightening of every muscle. Lauren concentrates on the movement of the peeler, as Spencer comes bounding in through the door.

'I heard about you,' he says. 'You're in for it.'

'Who told you?'

Spencer is trying to get his trainers off without untying the laces. 'Those boys in the football team.'

'Why would they talk to you?'

THE NEXT INSTALMENT

'Well, they didn't really *talk* to me. More like one of them pointed at me and shouted something about my sister being a thief.'

Lauren's face drains of colour.

'You tell them straight, Lauren. We ain't thieves. No one in my family takes what don't belong to them. That's what I said. We don't, do we?'

Something her mother says floats into her head.

'What's done can't be undone.'

Lauren halves the potatoes, boils water, pricks sausages. When Amber and Spencer are asleep she'll gather up their clothes for the washing machine, catch up with the ironing. Dread claws at her stomach the whole time. Mrs Lavender's kind face haunts her. She will never trust Lauren again, not after this. Why should she?

All the money Lauren earns goes into the old shoebox in the bottom of her wardrobe. There were forty pounds there last Sunday morning. The deadline for the next instalment was the following day. She spent the afternoon at Mrs Lavender's. The old lady had taught her to weed carefully. She said she knew she could trust Lauren to get things right.

Well, she hadn't got things right this time, had she?

That day, when Lauren arrived home, she found her mother on one end of the settee and a man she'd never seen before on the other. They were both in no condition for a conversation.

'Mum?'

Lauren's mother smiled. Then frowned.

'Had to do it, Lauren. Had to.'

'Do what, Mum?'

'So lonely, Lauren. Had to do it.'

'What, Mum? What did you have to do?'

'Pay you back. Soon.'

Lauren gasped; went straight to her wardrobe.

The shoe box lay open on the floor. Two ten-pound notes had gone.

'NO!' The sound came from deep inside Lauren. Her whole body seemed to scream. She heard someone stumble to the front door. When she went back into the living room, the man had gone.

'Mum, I want it back now. Do you understand? NOW.'

Lauren's mother looked blankly at her.

In the kitchen, Lauren slumped in the corner, her shoulders shaking with sob after sob. She imagined her mother that morning, finally getting out of bed. Maybe she was out of cigarettes. Maybe she felt the blackness of a depression coming on. Or simply the craving for a drink. And this week's money was all spent. Gone. But Mum knew her daughter had some money somewhere. It wouldn't have taken her long to find it.

Lauren stood up. Grinding one hand against the other, she strode into the living room.

'That was my money, my trip money. You stole my money, Mum.'

Lauren stopped. Her mother's eyes were glazed.

'Lauren?'

'Oh what's the point...'

Lauren spent the rest of the day like a zombie, trying to work out what to do. She called Kerry, her truest friend. Pouring her heart out, she ended with a whisper.

'There's no way I can get twenty quid by tomorrow.'

'Listen, Lauren,' said Kerry, 'Why don't you ask Miss Carraway for a bit more time.'

'Do you think she'll...'

'Yes, course she will. She's not a bad old stick. She'll understand.'

Lauren had spent all Sunday evening concocting a story that would sound plausible when she went to see Miss Carraway. In the end she thought her brother needing new shoes sounded the best. Totally unselfish. Miss Carraway would only have to imagine the poor boy's feet crushed into his old shoes, corns and blisters popping up all over the place.

Miss Carraway gave Lauren till the end of the week.

'I need to do something drastic,' she told her friend.

On Tuesday after school, Lauren went along to Mrs Lavender's. All she had to do was wait until the old lady asked if she would make a cup of tea. Mrs Lavender kept her money in the kitchen. It was easy really. The purse was opened. Two ten-pound notes were removed. The purse was closed. Lauren stuffed the money into her jeans pocket.

'I'm paying it back,' Lauren told herself. Then a small voice in her head whispered that the old lady probably wouldn't miss it anyway.

The £40 was given in at school on Wednesday morning.

After lunch on Friday, Lauren was summoned to the headteacher's office. 'It has come to my attention...'

Lauren froze to the spot. Kerry. Kerry had told on her.

The headteacher was serious, his tone cold. He was 'utterly appalled that someone like Lauren...'

She began to cry.

There were questions. Yes, she had taken money. From Mrs Lavender. Yes, she knows she is a thief.

'I'm going to pay it back,' she sobbed.

'I shall make sure you do.'

There is to be a meeting at school on Monday. Lauren is given a letter to take home, inviting her mother to come along too.

Now her brother Spencer will know she is a thief. The whole school too. Kerry won't speak to her; won't reply to her texts. How stupid she was to confide in her friend about what she's done. All because of that stupid pact. 'No buts' had become their motto. No buts. I always tell you everything. You can trust what I say.

Monday comes, and Lauren has not shown her mother the letter. The morning drags by. Lauren spends lunch time in the library, hunched over a book she isn't reading. At two o'clock she is sent for.

'Your mother's not here yet,' says the school secretary. 'She's coming, isn't she?'

Lauren shakes her head.

The secretary ushers the terrified girl into the room where the headteacher and Mrs Lavender are waiting. Lauren cannot look at the old lady.

'What have you to say for yourself?'

In the silent room, Lauren can hear boys on the distant football field, the phone ringing in the office, the clock ticking.

Mrs Lavender leans forward slightly.

'Lauren. We have been friends for quite a time, haven't we? Would you please talk about why you came to do jobs for me.'

Mrs Lavender speaks softly and kindly. Lauren feels worse. She expected an angry confrontation.

Lauren looks at the carpet, and clears her throat.

'I wanted to go to France,' she says. She stops. It all seems such a wasted effort now. How could she ever have had dreams of talking to real French people in their own language, of studying at university, maybe becoming a teacher herself one day?

It is Mrs Lavender who takes up her story, who speaks so kindly of her, telling the headteacher how she cares for Amber and Spencer, and for her mother too.

'My mother has a weakness,' says Lauren defensively. 'She's not well.'

Mrs Lavender agrees, and Lauren looks up at her with surprise.

'She needs help,' the old lady says quietly.

This is not the way people usually speak about her mother.

Mrs Lavender goes on. She asks Lauren what became of the money she earned. All that weeding and dusting. All that Sprogg-walking.

'The truth now, Lauren.'

And this is it. The moment she has dreaded all her life. When she has to tell someone what her mum is really like. She bites the side of her thumb.

No-one moves.

When Lauren speaks, her words are interspersed with things like, 'She's a good mum inside,' and, 'She's kind to us,' and, 'She's sorry she's got the weakness.'

And at last Lauren breaks free of this burden of silence, of covering up what she knows is true. Her mother is an alcoholic.

Then Mrs Lavender says that she will help look after Lauren, Spencer and Amber if Lauren's mum will agree to treatment. She says the missing £20 is a gift, gladly given to her friend, Lauren.

'I'd like to speak to Kerry too.'

That's one thing even Mrs Lavender can't sort out, surely.

'She came to see me at the weekend, Lauren. She told me I could trust you. Totally. No buts.'

Lauren swallows.

No buts.

She wants to say thank you but she can't speak.

Lauren looks at Mrs Lavender, and weeps.

The Whole-Face Smile

Rachael puts the phone down as carefully as she can in the circumstances. She bites her lip. Why does her mother have to be so opinionated, especially about this?

'Mu.'

She turns to see Nicky looking at her, his little face so trusting, his tongue lolling, too big for his mouth. Rachael holds out her arms and cuddles him. She wants to shelter him from all that is bad in the world. She carries him into the kitchen, slides him into his high chair.

'Time for a drink, love.'

'I'm sure he'll get there in the end,' her mother said. Of course she couldn't help crowing about her other two grandchildren, and they couldn't help being child prodigies and future Olympic champions. Stop it, Rachael tells herself. Your mother is only concerned about you. She loves Nicky, you know that.

Do I know it? Her inner self clamours angrily.

'Biscuit,' she says, holding out a chocolate finger. Nicky doesn't need language to tell her how delighted he is. Perhaps he'll settle down at preschool soon. The ladies were so apologetic when she told them Nicky had learnt to pinch in the first week he was there.

'What would you like? Apple juice? Orange? Milk?'

Nicky smiles with his whole face.

'Mu,' he says. It's his only word so far, but he isn't four yet, and he does understand a lot.

Rachael talks to Nicky while she makes her coffee. She chants their favourite rhymes. Nicky claps his hands. In a place deep inside her head, Rachael inspects the latest conversation with her mother. A week ago she'd hinted that she and Simon were trying for another baby.

'Are you sure this is sensible?' was the response. 'Personally, I don't think it's worth the risk.'

'What risk is that?' Rachael asked bravely.

'Well, dear, if you've had one, there must be a strong possibility that you'll have another.

Could you really manage two Down's Syndrome children?'

Now her mother has consulted the internet. She'd sounded fierce, and panicky.

'You're almost forty, Rachael. It's a dangerous age. You must take the sensible path. Give up all thoughts of another child. Concentrate on the one you've been given. I'm thinking of you dear, of your own mental health, of your marriage to Simon. Follow the safest option, for all our sakes.'

A week passes. Since the pinching episode, Rachael has stayed at preschool with Nicky. She sees how well he relates to other children with his cheery face and gentle ways, how he enjoys their company. He would love a younger sibling. Simon is more than keen, waiving away all opposition as if it matters not a jot. He suggests inviting Rachael's mother to come and stay for the weekend. Seeing them again may put her mind at rest, convince her they are happy; that they wouldn't swap Nicky for any other child in the world; that they are ready to extend their family.

Thus, when Simon is digging in the garden, his trusty helper beside him, wielding a plastic spade, Rachael's mother sits peeling potatoes. The clock ticks. She speaks out of the loud silence.

'You're thirty-nine, Rachael. A mother's age makes a difference in these matters.'

'I know that, Mum.' Rachael is mixing stuffing for the chicken. 'The doctor assured me I'd be very unlucky to have another child like Nicky.'

'There you are then.'

'I told him I wouldn't regard myself as unlucky. I would feel blessed.' Rachael's hands begin to shake, but outwardly she is calm.

Her mother sighs. 'My darling girl,' she says, 'don't let your own selfishness mislead you.'

'As it has in the past, you mean, don't you? I will never be sorry we refused the amniocentesis test. Look out of the window, Mum. Nicky's the sweetest, gentlest child imaginable. He won't ever emulate his talented cousins, but he'll always make people happy.'

Her mother nods slowly. 'It took some getting used to, his condition, I'll admit that. He is delightful, I know. But I'm not talking about Nicky, love. I'm talking about holding on to what you have, a happy child, a contented husband. You are preparing to choose a very stressful path. Think about it. Please.'

'Simon wants another child, too.' Rachael sounds petulant. She opens the oven door. A blast of hot air hits her face, like a reprimand.

She suppresses her fury as she makes coffee, puts biscuits onto a plate, takes out Nicky's non-spill mug. She looks at her mother, expecting anger, but all she sees is sorrow.

Two months go by. Nicky says 'Da' for the first time. He stays at preschool on his own. The family is spending the weekend with Rachael's mother. Rachael and Simon have something to tell her, and they want to do it face to face. Simon says she'll be fine, but Rachael's not convinced.

In the park, Granny pushes Nicky on the swings, then sits and watches as Rachael follows his amble amongst the children. A sudden commotion on the helter-skelter slide has everyone turning their heads. A boy of about seven is hurtling downwards. The bag he was carrying has burst, and marbles are bouncing and scattering around him.

Nicky is amazed, delighted. He stoops to gather up some of the little glass spheres. The boy lands on the ground, shouts, 'Oy, you.' Nicky goes towards him, smiling, holding out the boy's treasure. The boy takes it, then Nicky goes sturdily off on his quest, eager to return the marbles to the boy, offering only help and friendship. The last few are retrieved from a brown puddle.

Rachael leads Nicky back to the park bench. Her mother is beaming with joy.

'Oh, Rachael, I am sorry,' she says. 'What a joy our Nicky is. My little star. I'm so proud of you.'

Rachael looks at Simon. The moment may be right.

Nicky puts a muddy hand on his Granny's knee.

'Ga,' he says, and he gives her a whole-face smile.

The Sign

I always get there early. I sort the books. I know the popular authors, the ones that will sell. Paperbacks mostly. I put the ones with brown pages into a box under the table. The ones with miniscule print. They're mostly old, the people who come to the coffee morning. First Saturday of the month. Church Hall. They don't say much to me, the regulars. I keep my head down. Besides, there's always something new on the book stall to deflect their attention. Phyllis on cakes brings books every time. Gives me a smile I can't return. The vicar's wife too. She gathers them up on her charitable missions.

It was the vicar's wife who asked me if I could come and help. After a suitable period had passed of course. She's a model of understanding, of compassion. It's too much to bear, all that sympathy, all that pity. I go home and weep. Mostly for myself. But for her too, that she can't get through to me, in spite of her well-meant efforts. And I weep for Gemma, five hundred miles away, putting on a brave face. I phone her. I have to brace myself every time.

'Mum,' she says, 'Are you OK?'

I'm not. But what can I say?

'Gemma,' I say quietly, 'Oh Gemma.'

We both weep soundlessly. She tells me about the primroses along the banks of the River Nairn, long after mine have faded here in the south west; about the dentist she works for; about the weather. I listen. I respond. She thanks me for phoning. I replace the receiver, and stare at the wallpaper. It's covered in green ferns, locked in unmoving swirls. The hall is silent.

'Customers,' calls Phyllis brightly, and they start coming in. Some of them used to be my friends. They don't know what to say to me any more. Joan touches my shoulder, but I don't acknowledge her. How can I, when her two grandchildren come scurrying after her, searching for Thomas the Tank and Rapunzel in the children's section.

I no longer have a stiff upper lip. Rather, I have no lip at all. I sit, and sometimes, without meaning to, I hear snatches of conversations from the coffee drinkers.

'It can't be easy.'

'Heaven alone knows we've all tried.'
'Poor soul.'
'She's had counselling, you know.'

Once I heard this. 'She should pull herself together.'

Limb by limb. If only I could.

I heard someone say I'd lost my faith. Must have noticed the seat where I always used to sit. Four rows back. Left hand side. No longer occupied. An empty space.

At first some of them called, bringing pies and flowers and leaflets about grief. Smiles. Their own messages of comfort. I said nothing. I felt nothing. For most of the time I live in the only space I can call my own. The space where no-one can reach me. I am not comfortable there. Yet I do not willingly move away from it. But sometimes I am dragged out, kicking, screaming, raving. Always at home, always alone.

I haven't lost my faith. I read the Bible every morning. I think of Amos, the shepherd, the one who tended his flocks under the sycamore trees. I see him, sitting under a sky full of stars, the gentle comfort of sheep, the occasional rustle. Plenty of time to think.

Let justice roll on like a river, and righteousness like a never-failing stream.

Justice. Is it justice that HE got four years? For what he did?

And as for righteousness, what's the point. When did righteousness ever end the suffering?

Gemma writes to me. Once a fortnight. I cannot bring myself to reply. Not in a letter. I cannot write down what I want to say. But Gemma writes. Her letters never fail to arrive.

She tells me not to dwell on things so much, to remember how kind I always was when they came to stay, cooking their favourite dinners, baking the chocolate cakes they loved so much. Those gingerbread men. Playing endless games with Jack. She tells me to remember the good times. The trips to the beach. The slide and the swings. But underneath all those positive thoughts written in that carefully controlled script, I read Gemma's anguish, her agony.

A letter came today, as I was leaving for the coffee morning. I have it in my pocket now. I'll save it for later, when I'm alone. I long to read it, and I dread reading it. It will bring back to me once more what happened, and I will know, once again, that it was my fault.

Two ladies are coming towards my stall. They're talking about the new sign at the edge of the village.

'It's ever so good,' says Ellen, 'If you're doing more than forty, a sign lights up all red and flashy. My Ted got quite a shock. Well you know what he's like. "Why go forty when you can get away with fifty?" he says.'

I can see Tina, the other one, out of the corner of my eye, looking at me nervously.

'I think it's very good,' she says.

Ellen starts to say something else, but Tina butts in.

'Ooh, look, a Maeve Binchy. I haven't read that one, have you?'

Why go forty when you can go fifty? Ellen's words burn into my brain. I am going to cry again. I reach into my bag for my handkerchief.

Tina and Ellen engross themselves in the blurb on the book's back cover. Tina whispers something, and Ellen nods. They are desperate to make the moments pass as normally as possible.

I force my thoughts out of this hall, with its stalls of hand-me-down clothes and home-made cards and neatly potted house plants. Cakes and flowers. These well-thumbed books. I force myself to think about Hosea. Something I read this morning.

I desire mercy, not sacrifice.

I look up at Ellen, forthright, down to earth, blunt, and Tina, sensitive, thoughtful, timid. I used to like them so much. Now I want to punish somebody. Anybody. Everybody. In the old days I had mercy to spare. Not any more.

I've seen the forty mile an hour light-up sign. I've walked past it already, on one of my pointless walks. Forty miles an hour. It's not much to ask is it, through our village? At least on the main road, down the hill, past the farm and the new houses. It's thirty on the side roads, twenty past the school. Forty's quite fast enough to take that bend. I know that if anyone does.

Ellen offers me her money wordlessly.

The vicar's wife brings me a cup of coffee.

On my way home I finger Gemma's letter in my pocket. Back in my kitchen I bring it out into the daylight.

I slide a finger under the envelope. The paper jags and rips. The letter is in my hand.

'Dear Mum.'

She can still say that then. I close my eyes. Yes, she means it. When it first happened, we were both numb. Silent. Unable to weep. After Gemma and Paul returned to Scotland I was consumed by grief. I was drowning in something and I couldn't fight it.

'Mum,' she writes, 'I had a letter from your vicar's wife yesterday, and she told me how empty you are feeling. I know you always try to hide this from me.'

I put the letter down. She's wrong. I don't feel empty any more. I did at first. Now I feel full. Of hate and rage and helplessness. And pushing its way in, I feel guilt. Most of the time I feel guilt. Because it was all my fault. Yes, all my fault. I was the one who was pushing the buggy. I was the one taking little Jack for a walk, while Gemma and Paul were at the art exhibition. I was the one talking to Jack, telling him we'd see the cows in the field, and it wasn't far from here. It was me who couldn't get him out of the way as the car came round the bend, tyres squealing, brakes slamming, wheels skidding. Me screaming. Jack's little body, crushed, lifeless, empty.

Little Jack. Such beautiful eyes. Such a wide smile.

I wish and wish that it was me who had been killed. Not Jack.

Now I want that driver to suffer as Jack suffered, as my daughter and her husband suffer, as I suffer. I want revenge, of huge biblical proportions, something more than a few years in prison. For that driver I want something mind-shattering, lasting, eternal. A painful and lingering kind of torment inflicted mercilessly.

This sheer hatred overpowers me, and then seesaws back to that terrible tsunami of guilt.

Hosea's words come gently back to me. Hosea, the man with the wayward wife, the man who knew about suffering and pain. And what surprised me so much about him... he knew forgiveness.

I desire mercy not sacrifice. That was God's message to Hosea.

I'm in automatic mode. I make myself a sandwich, take it into the garden. It's overgrown now, but it hides me from the world. I hear a bird singing. The rambling rose is full of buds. Suddenly I know. All this hatred, this wish for revenge has not been punishing the murderer who killed my grandson. He hasn't been affected by that at all. But I have. I have been punishing myself.

Mercy not sacrifice. For so long I have wanted that man to make some sort of huge never-ending sacrifice, and in the end it wasn't him making it, it was me. I have been sacrificing my life when I should have been praying for the gift of mercy.

The garden seat needs cleaning and repainting, but I sit on it anyway. I bite into my sandwich. I watch a bee climbing out of a flower, laden with pollen. Jack used to love insects.

I am wondering whether to put on my gardening clothes, find a fork, dig up the weeds. The latch on the garden gate clicks, and there's Tina.

'Fancy a cream tea?'

I hesitate.

'There's a new place opened near Looe,' she says. 'I feel like a trip. Cheer myself up after that nasty flu. It leaves you feeling a bit weak, a bit vulnerable. I don't want to go on my own. Do come. My car's outside.'

We drive out of the village, along lanes sleepy with sunshine. We pass that little pub I went to with my family, the one with the playground and the dinosaur slide Jack loved so much. My daughter's right. It's good to remember the happy times. They carry their own kind of mercy, those memories.

Tina's good company. The cream tea is perfect – home-made scones and runny strawberry jam. The cottage garden is crammed with flowers. Geraniums and roses. Lavender. There are bees and butterflies, and I think about Jack again.

I'd have gone a different way that day, if I'd known. Of course I would. Of course I'd have saved him if I could. To me he was the most beautiful and special child in the world. Any grandparent will know how I feel.

We drive home. At the entrance to the village we approach the new forty miles an hour reminder sign. And then, right then, as I'm bracing myself against the pain, Tina thanks me for coming, and says I've made her feel a whole lot better.

She hasn't slowed enough. The sign lights up, flashes. 40.40.40.

'Whoops, sorry,' she says. She brakes.

I find I'm thinking of Jack and the cows, how he loved them, reaching out his podgy hands and laughing with joy. Such joy.

'I don't suppose that driver will ever be the same,' I say, 'knowing what he's done.'

Mercy not sacrifice. Jack. One day I'll be able to think of him with a smile.

Stargazing

An overview. That's what I've got now. An overview. I bet that makes you smile, even on a day like today.

You know, I've always had a calling for open spaces and clear bright skies, haven't I? In the daylight of course. Dad used to take us out to Dartmoor, didn't he? He'd open the car door and we'd run and run. Remember that time you lay down in the heather? Flat out on the ground. You'd completely disappeared as far as he was concerned. Staring about in disbelief he was.

'Where's Matt?' he boomed.

Wanted to know if I'd seen you go. He couldn't understand why I thought it was so funny. I couldn't speak – what with the laughter and the stitch from trying to keep up with you. Then of course he started bellowing your name into the wind, and I could tell he wasn't going to get the joke. Not the way I told it anyway. You somehow managed it though, didn't you? You popped up out of the undergrowth and calmed him down, brought a smile to his face. You could always do that, couldn't you?

Those moors. Do you remember the time he took us out there one night? I didn't want to go, not one little bit. Dad said I was being selfish.

'As usual.'

Those were his words. He must have known you'd told me all those stories of the Hound of the Baskervilles and The Beast That Roams.

'Matt needs to try out his telescope in the darkest place we can find,' Dad said.

'Hawaii's the darkest place on earth.' I was trying to impress Dad with my knowledge. He'd always liked it when we told him things. He wasn't in the mood that time.

'Do you know how far away Hawaii is?' He sounded a bit fierce. He used that voice, you know, when you think you've done something wrong but you're not sure what it is.

Anyway, we went up to the moor. I didn't want to get out of the car, what with the darkness and The Beast. You were hopping about while Dad set up your telescope. Shouting to me to come out and look at the stars. I've seen stars before, I thought crossly.

'Let her stay there if she wants to,' said Dad. That's what did it. Dad saying that. I forced myself to get out of the car before I'd counted to ten. By that time you were peering through the telescope, and Dad was pointing excitedly. I shut the car door very quietly, because loud noises could attract anything roaming those moors. Anything. I peered about, straining my eyes. Then I looked up.

'Wow.' The word was out before I could stop it. So many stars. Everywhere. Layered throughout the sky. I took a quick look around. No signs of Beast movement. It didn't seem quite so dark now. The moor rolled away into the distance. Everywhere was quiet. There was a tor not far from us, massive against the beautiful sky.

'Look up.' Dad sounded tetchy. I expect he thought I wasn't interested.

'Can I have a go, Matt?' I said. 'Please.'

'In a minute,' you said. Well, it was your present, and you had read all those books about astronomy.

When it was my turn, I nearly spoiled it, didn't I? Maybe you don't remember. I wanted to look at the moon first, to see if the face really was made of craters. But at the same time, I was still worrying about The Beast. I'm not blaming you for all the stories you'd told me. I loved them. Even the scary ones. I just wanted someone to keep watch while I looked at the moon. Dad said I was being silly. I don't think he ever understood what makes me tick.

Now I'm up here, and I can look at our little blue planet rotating so regularly, so determinedly, in our galaxy. Sometimes I long for my whole life to start spinning all over again.

Anyway, I can easily remember the journey home from the moors that night. You were bursting with all the things you'd seen. You were old enough to talk to Dad about constellations and galaxies. I stared out of the car window, remembering how the surface of the moon looked through your telescope. Not like rocks or sand, but sort of silky and welcoming.

Dad tried taking us out again, didn't he? But the second time I really blew it. That scream.

'Enough to waken the dead.'

Dad's words again. How was I to know that the dark shadow moving softly towards us was only a pony. Only a pony. You and your stories, Matt.

I think I only became a scientist because of you. And Dad I suppose. Even now I'm reluctant to give him any of the credit. Dad always thought of you as the clever one. He was so proud of you. I seem to have spent my whole life wanting him to feel the same way about me.

He really missed you when you went off to university. He couldn't stop himself talking about you and what you were doing. He hardly seemed to notice me, tagging along in your footsteps. I had to work hard to achieve half of what you did so easily. After you left home, I spent hours in my room.

'Listening to music again,' Dad would say. He had no idea.

Then later, when you did your PhD, and I had my place at somewhere that wasn't Oxford or Cambridge, Dad did seem satisfied. I hadn't let the side down. I'd done my best.

Then there was your research to talk about. Whenever I came home, that was Dad's favourite topic of conversation. He loved to tell everyone all about it. How ironic that it's cancer cells that occupy your days. How terrible that Dad's illness came so suddenly, before you or anyone else could find a cure, or at least find some way of stopping the spread of his tumours. It must have broken your heart. You were always so close.

I don't know how I was ever chosen for the programme. You could hardly believe I'd volunteered, and as for Dad...

'You'll hate it,' he said.

But you knew, didn't you? I remember your smile.

'She'll be orbiting the skies, Dad. Closer to the moon than you or I will ever go.'

'Madness,' he said.

'At least there aren't any Beasts or Hounds up there,' you said.

Dad looked at me.

'Why don't you just grow up. Get married. Settle down. Have some kids.'

At that moment I knew. Dad didn't want me to be as clever as you; didn't want me to pass exams with stars and distinctions. He didn't need another genius in the family, because he had you. All he wanted from me was this. To be a good little girl who would grow up to marry someone very suitable, and then go on to produce his grandchildren.

Oh, Matt, I got it all wrong. And now here I am orbiting the world in the space station; one of the few chosen astronauts; envied by children the world over.

I let him down so many times. Often I didn't know why. Now I'm as respected in the scientific world as you are. But for Dad, it must have been yet another let down.

I'm sorry about today, Matt. That you have to go to Dad's funeral on your own. I want to be with you so much. Because I understand. I know you so well. You'll be thinking that at the end it was you who let him down, because you couldn't discover some way of keeping his cancer in remission. You couldn't beat it in time to save him. Or at least till I got back. So he could have us both there. So he could see at last that I wasn't just tiresome and a nuisance. So he could see me as I really am. His caring daughter who has always tried so hard to please him.

A six month tour of duty is a long time.

That stargazing has a lot to answer for, Matt. That's where Dad put you. Up with the stars. So proud of you. Of your achievements. You know, all that time I didn't want to be just like you, Matt. I wanted to *be* you. And all Dad wanted was a girl. A daughter.

It can be lonely up here, Matt, in spite of friends and colleagues, in spite of the hard work, in spite of the jokes. I've had a lot of time to think.

Actually, Matt, I've met someone. Here in the satellite. You'll like him. I wish Dad could meet him too. Then he'd know. It's not too late for some of his dreams for me to come true.

A Bit of Peace and Quiet

Early morning by the river. Tamar sits motionless, watching, waiting. Good job the boys aren't up yet, she thinks. They'd be hurling themselves at the water, drenching each other, calling to her. 'Come on in.' 'Don't be a spoil sport.' Things like that. Which is all very well when she feels like it. If only they wouldn't gang up on her so much. She sighs. If only she'd been put with a different family.

On the far bank a brick-red tail undulates along a branch as a squirrel flips through the trees. Tamar's father comes out of the tent, yawning, stretching; a towel over one shoulder.

'Dad, you've still got your pyjamas on. Embarrassing or what?'

Her father laughs, and wanders off to the wash-rooms. Tamar knows she hasn't got much longer to sit here alone, breathing in the morning, watching the river. Three dragonflies hover and dart: bright blue sticks against the flow of the weeds.

'Yeee-hi!'

Ben bursts out of the pup tent. He's wearing his swimming costume. He starts dragging the dinghy towards the river. Tamar watches a crowd of pond-skaters flash away. Then Ben's crashing into the water. He turns to flick handfuls at his older sister.

'Stop it, you little pest!' Tamar gets to her feet as her mother's rebuke comes sharply out of the tent. 'Don't start.'

Tamar sticks out her tongue. Ben tries to splash her again, but by now she's too far away.

After breakfast Mum, Dad and the boys want to go canoeing. Tamar assures them she'll be OK on her own, but Mum doesn't want to leave her.

'I am thirteen,' she says.

The boys are teasing each other, arguing about who's the better canoeist. Ben whacks Rob over the head to emphasize his point, and world war three threatens to break out.

'She did hate canoeing the other day,' says Dad. 'Stop it, you two.'

'I'll stay on the camp-site, Mum,' says Tamar, 'and I won't run off with strangers. I promise.'

Mum relents. 'You could wash up for us, then we can make an early start. And don't look like that. A sullen frown isn't pretty, you know.'

'Fish face,' says Ben when his mother's not listening. 'Moody-moo.'

After they've gone, Tamar fills the washing up bowl with the dishes, and carries it to the sink area. She has to pass three chalets on her way. They have white furniture inside, and sun-loungers outside, with deep blue cushions. Tamar would love to sit there all morning. She could read, rub sun-cream on her arms and watch the children playing.

In one of the chalets, a man is eating breakfast; a lady in a long white sun-dress sips orange juice. Tamar wants to look like that when she's older. Chic.

On her way back with the clean dishes, the lady is by herself, just sitting, hands in her lap, staring down at her plate.

Tamar goes back to the tent. The family next door call to her, and she stops to chat. They don't think she's sullen or moody. They're going to the swimming pool. Would she like to join them? Tamar smiles. At least these children are too small to duck her under the water, and so far they've been friendly, haven't called her names, or laughed and said she's a wimp.

After playing in the pool for an hour the smallest child is tired. Tamar offers to get changed and push the toddler round the campsite in her buggy. The mother is grateful.

'An hour's peace,' she says. 'Heaven.'

Tamar pushes the buggy, and the little girl makes cooing noises and waves her arms about. They take the route past the chalets. The lady is standing in the doorway now, her hands round a mug. She has long dark hair; Tamar thinks she looks like Kate, as in William and Kate. Tamar stops for a moment and the lady smiles.

'Hello. Going for a walk?'

'Yes.'

'Your sister?'

'No, she's our neighbour. I'm getting her to sleep.'

The toddler starts rocking backwards and forwards.

'I think she wants to move on,' says the lady. 'May I come with you?'

'I'm not going far.'

'That's fine. I'd like to join you. Take my mind off things.'

The Kate look-alike puts her mug on the table, picks up her handbag, zip-fastens the door. Her name's Jemima. They walk along, chatting about the Dordogne, the weather, the swimming pool. Jemima asks about Tamar's family. Has she got any brothers and sisters? Do they all get on? Where are they today?

By the time they reach the camp shop, the toddler is asleep. Jemima buys enormous ice-creams. They sit on a bench to eat them.

'Jemima, where's your husband this morning?' Tamar knows he's not ill in bed, because she saw him eating breakfast.

'Oh,' sighs Jemima, 'he wants to be on his own today.'

'I like being on my own,' says Tamar.

A weary smile passes over Jemima's face. 'I'm not surprised, from what you've said about your brothers.'

'Sometimes I get up before they do, and I sit by the river.' She pauses. 'It's great when it's quiet. There's a kingfisher, some-one told us. I'd like to see it.'

'I'd love to see a kingfisher,' says Jemima. 'Would you mind if I join you tomorrow? I know where your tent is.'

They walk slowly round the camp-site. A few children play on the swings; the swimming pool is busy. A lady in a red sundress comes along the path towards them, a girl of about four tugging on her arm. As they pass, the lady shakes the child off.

'Do stop prattling for a minute, can't you?'

Jemima and Tamar look at each other.

'I can't have children,' says Jemima.

'Why not?'

'I've had lots of tests. There's something wrong with my insides.'

Tamar doesn't know what to say. She's a bit worried this lady might start to tell her a lot of grown-up stuff she won't understand.

'I'm thirteen,' she says, thinking that might help.

Jemima looks down at the sleeping child in the buggy. 'I shall never be a mother.'

Tamar frowns. 'You could adopt a baby.'

Jemima's face changes. 'No.' She pauses. 'You don't know what you'd be getting, do you?'

'I'm adopted,' says Tamar. She is anxious to get this aired before Jemima says anything she shouldn't.

'Are you? Gosh, your parents were lucky to get you, weren't they?'

'They don't always think so.' Tamar manoeuvres the buggy round a corner.

'Really?'

Tamar can remember times she's got on her mum's nerves. She thinks of the lady they met on the path, the child skipping along, chatting happily, being told to stop prattling.

'Your brothers are quite a handful,' says Jemima. 'I wouldn't like that.'

'You could choose a girl,' says Tamar eagerly. 'My mum and dad chose me.'

Jemima looks thoughtful. 'Your parents chose a sweet little girl, but then they chose your brothers. Two boisterous boys,' she says.

'My brothers aren't *too* bad,' says Tamar. She wants Jemima to like children. 'Besides, Mum and Dad didn't choose them. They just arrived, I'm afraid.'

'What?'

'When I was three, they were getting ready to choose a sister for me. Mum found out she was going to have a baby.'

'Really?'

'Yes.'

'Actually, my whole family's very sporty and I'm not. I do love them, but sometimes I wish I'd ended up in another place.'

'There are probably a lot of people who wish that,' says Jemima. 'Not just adopted people either. Anyway, it's not a bad thing, you know. You're just different from them. You are exactly who you should be. For example, do they know much about birds?'

Tamar laughs and shakes her head.

They stop outside Jemima's chalet.

'Would you like some lemonade?' she asks.

Tamar takes the toddler back to her mother, then runs as fast as she can along the path. She doesn't want Jemima to forget about the lemonade. But there it is, ready on the small table between the sun-loungers.

Jemima and Tamar sit together and talk about the things they like, favourite colours, meals, songs. They're trying to remember the words of a song they both know, singing and stopping, singing and breaking into giggles, when a man comes round the corner. He frowns at them.

'This is Jacob, my husband,' says Jemima. 'Jake, this is Tamar, from one of the tents by the river.'

The man nods; gives a brief smile.

'Shall I go?' asks Tamar.

'No. Finish your lemonade.'

The air is hot and still; a child comes running by, hair dripping, flip-flops slapping the path. But something has changed.

Tamar watches as the two adults eye each other. She's seen her mum and dad like this, when they're tired from work, and there are jobs to be done, the bins to put out, the washing machine to empty; when she and her brothers have been fighting.

'Tamar was adopted,' says Jemima gently. The man stares at Tamar, and suddenly she understands. It's not the lady who doesn't want to adopt a child; it's the man. She sips her drink, feeling awkward.

'I suppose those wild boys are adopted too.' Jacob makes Tamar feel personally responsible for their behaviour.

'They're just excited to be here,' she says, and then she stops, and looks at Jemima. They smile at each other. 'My brothers aren't adopted. Just me.'

The man looks surprised. He goes into his chalet. He comes back looking thoughtful, a beer in his hand.

'My dad likes beer,' says Tamar. She looks away, thinking about grown-ups and their crossness – this man, Jacob; her mother; the lady in red, the one who snapped at her little girl. Maybe all mothers get like that sometimes, desperate for a bit of peace and quiet. That's something to remember.

She thanks Jemima. 'I'd better go.'

'Don't forget, tomorrow morning. At the river bank.'

Jacob looks at the two of them, a question unspoken on his face. Jemima explains about the kingfisher.

'Early morning by the river.' Tamar looks at Jacob, and smiles. 'You can come too, if you like.'

Mr Wacker's Bridge

A plastic bag flutters against the railings. A can rolls towards the river. A horn gives a mournful sigh, and water laps the concrete wall.

The boy walks, one foot in front of the other. No-where to go. Eighteen years old today, and all he gets is complaints and criticism. They call him Teddy at home and he hates it. They call him Edward at school and he hates that too. He stares at the pavement; the chewing gum, the pigeon droppings, the rubbish. They just about sum up his life.

He peers at the river; sniffs its slight mustiness. The usual late evening lights flicker and dance in the flow. Then there's the same old blackness, swirling, slapping, almost chuckling against the side of the boring grey walkway.

A couple approach him, arms round each other. She's talking; he's nodding. Non-complicated lives. Why do some people strike lucky?

Ahead there's a bridge. The boy stops, unsettled by what he sees. He waits, motionless, a thin figure in a hoodie, curving away from his own height. There's a group of them ahead. Old mostly. One's nodding. Looks as if there's a conversation going on in his head, and he's desperate to keep up. Another one's lips move, muttering to himself, eyes closed. And the Edward part of the boy recognises his need: beyond the traffic's perpetual thrust, there's a threatening silence.

The boy's never walked this far before. He's seen homeless people, of course, walked by them in the street, never really thought much about them. The part of him that answers to Teddy wants to run away. In case. In case they're like his father was, or his mother's ex, or his mother's present partner. Alf. He's the worst. Makes the boy cower; makes him into a nobody.

'University? Geology? What's the use of that? You want to study stones, your mother can get you a few in the park.' Alf's laughter is cruel, derisive. 'And who'd'ya think's going to pay for you to go off to some crackpot university? It's about time you went out and found a job. Teddy.'

The boy knows why he hates that name. It's because when Alf says it, he feels as if he's a child's soft toy that's been hurled out of the pram. And trodden on.

He clenches his fists; watches the group of rough-looking men. The one in the knitted balaclava tosses a bit of old cloth on the brazier. Sparks lift and fall. A flame leaps and dies. The boy is not close enough to smell the harsh mix of cigarette smoke and smouldering fabric, but he imagines them. There'll be pigeons, too, in the roof of the bridge, huddling together, shuffling nervously.

The boy shivers. November's a bleak month.

A woman arrives, dirty brown mac, hands in fingerless gloves. She's carrying newspapers. She shares out the pages. She helps the mumbling chap stuff some down the front of his coat. No-one grabs. Civilisation clings, even in this outpost.

Something's happening. A van pulls up on the bridge, honks once. The man in the balaclava moves swiftly among the others, rousing them from torpor. The woman helps the nodding one to his feet, and up they go, up the steps, slowly, their faces set against the wind.

Balaclava Man goes last. Before he puts his foot on the steps, he turns, looks in Edward's direction, jerks his head towards the van.

'Come on,' he calls in a flat voice. Edward looks round. There's no-one behind him. Is the man gesturing to him?

'Yeah, you.'

At the top of the steps, there are plastic cups of soup, tomato with something else. The adjectives 'warming' and 'nourishing' float into Edward's head.

'Thank you,' he says, fighting tears.

Alf doesn't rule the world after all.

They sip in silence. The woman dishing up the soup offers a refill. It's astonishing, that such a polite society should exist in the dark forgotten places of the city. Edward knows it isn't all like this. There are people who would mug him for the few pounds he has in his pockets, leave him battered and bleeding on the pavement.

After he's drunk his soup, Balaclava Man heads off down the steps, and Edward follows him.

'Thank you,' he says again.

The fire is almost out now. A chill seeps up from the dark water.

'Run out of fags,' says the man. The boy's not sure what he means. The man resumes his place by the brazier. The boy stands there, shuffles nervously.

The one who nods wraps himself in a blanket; the mutterer huddles in a thin mac. The bottoms of his trousers are tied with string. The woman carries an old eiderdown over, sits down next to him, and covers them both.

The boy thinks he should move on, but he feels safe here.

At last Balaclava Man speaks.

'Run away, have you?'

The boy swallows.

'What's your name, son?'

Edward shakes his head. Son. The word brings a tremble to the boy's lip.

I don't like my name,' he mumbles, and he hears the distant voice of Alf shouting, 'Speak up will you.' And his poor mother saying, 'Do as he says, Ted.'

'No name,' mutters the man. He may be angry for all the boy knows. Edward/Teddy stands, silent, afraid.

'Wacker,' says the man suddenly. Edward is sure this can't be some sort of swearword he hasn't heard before, because Alf knows every single one that anybody has ever invented. The man holds out a grimy hand. Edward shakes it.

'Look like a Tom to me.'

'I'd like to be Tom, Mr Wacker.'

Wacker rubs his hands together. He doesn't suddenly yell, or sneer, or say, "Who asked for your opinion?' He doesn't hold a fist to the boy's chin, and ask, 'Did somebody say something? Or did a worm crawl in from the garden?'

Wacker smiles, coughs. 'No need for the title,' he says. 'Sit. Talk about yourself, Tom.'

Where should he start? With Alf's view that he's an idle layabout? With the fear he reads in his mother's eyes? With his own dread?

'I'd like to go to university,' he says.

Wacker doesn't laugh.

'What's stopping you, son?'

The boy is thoughtful. Teddy would know it was Alf; Edward would say it was the money.

'What does Tom say?' asks Wacker.

There is a pause. The fire has gone out. There is nothing but a damp chill in the air, something that forewarns of the bite of winter.

'You want this life, Tom?' Wacker jerks his head towards his companions. Tom looks away, bites his lip.

'All young once,' says Wacker. He closes his eyes for a second, concentrates. Tom understands the effort this man is making. 'You don't have to be what they say you'll be,' he says. 'Tom? I was, um, a bit like you, lad. But me, not clever enough. Not for university. Not enough to outwit them either.' He looks at Tom. 'Are you?'

Tom begins to cry. That's his problem. He's just Teddy, the wimp. Too scared to answer back. And Edward's not much better. His teachers say he works hard; he does all his assignments; he gets reasonable marks. But they never know what he's thinking.

'I've had it, Mr Wacker. I'm a lost cause.'

They sit together in silence – the boy on the verge of manhood, and the man who half-wishes he was a boy and could start again.

'You can do it,' whispers Wacker.

The boy shakes his head.

'Yes, you can.'

'You don't know me.'

'Know enough,' says Wacker. 'Go home. Stick it out. It can't be much longer. How old are you?'

'Eighteen today.'

Wacker coughs. Or is he laughing?

'Happy birthday.' And then he says, 'Want you to remember this day for the rest of your life, Tom.'

The boy looks doubtful.

'Have a birthday present from Wacker.' He holds an imaginary sword. 'Hereby name you, Sir Tom.'

The former Teddy/Edward can't help smiling. It's as if Wacker is offering him a chance.

He'll take it. In seven months he can leave. With any luck he'll get a couple of As, maybe a B. He might find a job, a holiday job perhaps. He might even take up that university place he's been offered.

He stands up; shakes the older man's hand.

'Be here if you need me,' says Wacker, the man who has nothing. 'Come. See me anytime, Tom. Don't let anyone, anyone, stand in your way.'

'I won't, sir,' says Tom. Wacker nods and sighs. Tom fumbles in his pocket, tries to give him all the money he has. But Wacker won't take it.

'I'll bring you some stuff,' says Tom, and he will. He strides away from a place he will always remember as Mr Wacker's Bridge.

A plastic bag flutters against the railings. A can rolls towards the river. A horn gives a mournful sigh, and water laps the concrete wall.

The Last Rays

I lie still and gaze at the sky. Am I here, on Exmoor? I pick out a planet, just as I did as a child on a frosty night in my father's fields, the cows safe in the barn. My mother would be in the kitchen, darning socks, or hemming my school skirt. She sometimes sang as she worked, songs she'd learnt from the wireless.

My eyes search the stars, and one of my mother's favourites comes gently into my head, and I see myself at fifteen, sixteen years old. I was the one with stars in my eyes, certain of my own wisdom, convinced that love would never make a fool of me.

Mother often laughed at me and my ambition. I wasn't going to stay here for ever, I said, watching bats as the day faded, listening to the owls hooting, running inside where the firelight flickered, and logs shifted in the hearth.

'I used to be like you,' she said, 'until I met your father.'

The moon's rising. You can see it from the city, but here on the moor, it's a well-remembered golden face, and it's almost smiling. I feel dizzy with the universe above me. There is so much of it, so many stars. Have they been here, all those years I spent away from them, all that time I could see so few of them? My father told me some of them might have died already. He said we might be seeing the last rays they will ever emit.

I didn't fall in love with a man, or a woman, for that matter, like they do nowadays. It wasn't another person that made a fool of me, but it was love. I wanted jazz bands and the theatre, the thud of feet at the changing of the guard, the slap of water under London Bridge. And people. Smart men in their suits and chic women dressed à la mode. I wanted to eat with them in stylish restaurants, go with them to exhibitions, discuss the latest plays. I had stars in my eyes, and I wanted everyone to see them.

After secretarial college, I found a job easily. A lot of us did in those days. My mother thought I'd soon come running home, tired of the smog, the rattle of the underground, cooking for myself on a tiny stove. But I didn't. It was the city that had me dancing on a string.

When I married Ken, he asked me if I wanted to move out to the suburbs, or maybe a village on the train line. He said he'd always had a yen to live somewhere quieter. I said no, I liked London too much to ever leave.

A few days ago, he confided that there were things he wished he'd done.

'What kind of things?' I asked.

'Oh, nothing important,' he said.

'Go on, tell me.'

He looked away, out of the window.

'Don't get me wrong,' he said. 'I've always loved you. You've been a wonderful wife, a marvellous mother. You have impeccable taste. You furnished our apartments almost single-handedly, especially when I was so busy. You never complained about all the entertaining we had to do.'

He paused, and I could see he was wondering whether to go on. He looked down at his hands, old now, the veins prominent.

'Tell me.'

'I wish I'd planted a rose garden, grown vegetables, mown a lawn. They say when you're old you only regret the things you didn't do.'

I wanted to hug him, remind him we'd done so many exciting things, been to some wonderful places. I wanted him to know I didn't regret a thing, not then, not at that moment.

'You've made my life perfect,' I said. And there was silence. He didn't reply.

Now, lying here on Exmoor, all that's coming back to me, and I know that Ken would have loved the country, and life in a village.

I look up, and I'm back to being a child, breathing in the scent of the hedgerows, hearing the distant bark of a fox.

We were happy, though, weren't we? Our three children wanted for nothing. They didn't exactly sail through their teenage years, but they've turned out all right.

I can hear my mother singing again, in the bitter-sweetness of Rosemary Clooney's voice, about the stars in my eyes, and being wise.

I did make him happy, I know I did. We bought pictures together, chose antiques, ate meals in expensive restaurants, took holidays by the sea.

Some-one is standing beside me, holding my hand. I have tears in my eyes, and I want it to be my mother, ready to lift me up to catch the scent of apple blossom, or pointing out a robin's nest in a grassy bank.

I hear a man singing the same song. Is it my father? He used to whistle the tune, but did he know the words? Is he talking about Ken and me? No, I want to say. You don't really think I had Ken dancing on a string, do you? I loved him, you know I did.

I want the farmhouse kitchen. I want the backdoor to open and my father to be there in his boots. I want my mother's arms about me, and I want her to forgive me.

I want my life back, and I can't have it.

I am sobbing, and a hand squeezes mine.

I can hear a humming noise, but all the bees are safe in their hives. I open my eyes, and there is no field, no dark sparkling sky.

There is only the white light of a hospital room.

Ken is holding my hand. Beyond him are our three beautiful children and their partners. Their faces are full of love and sadness.

'I got something right after all,' I whisper.

'You got most things right.' Ken's cheeks are damp.

'Buy a house in the country,' I whisper. 'Grow vegetables. Mow the lawn. Plant roses, and think of me.'

He bites his lip, and nods.

Rainbow Laughter

It's not the same any more. Life's galloping on and Arthur feels he's standing there in his slippers begging it to stop.

He can hear the people next door, their merriment, their gregariousness. That's how he recognises them. By the sound of their laughter. He gives them colours in his mind. The father's is a chocolate-brown belly-laugh. It rumbles over the fence. The mother's is the tinkle of blue glass, like one of those hanging mobiles jingling carelessly. The girls giggle, a bubbly brook of sound that gurgles over pink pebbles. The boys yelp and tease. They hoot and snort. That's indigo; invasive.

There's a toddler, too. Giggles and chortles and shouts and screams. Her colours clash. They're unpredictable.

Arthur sits in the conservatory. They've got their friends in, or possibly those wild relatives again. Probably both. The smell of something spicy drifts over the fence, leaks in through the windows. Dorothy used to like cooking; trying her hand at all sorts of dishes.

Arthur looks at the rocking chair. Dorothy's special place. He remembers her there so well, a ball of wool at her feet, knitting away, pausing to read the pattern, then gathering needles and yarn into a neat package, to go and make the tea. Always a ready smile for him. Dorothy. Arthur's eyes fill with tears. His shoulders shake. Two years, and it isn't getting any better.

The phone rings. Arthur stands up, blows his nose. He crosses the room.

'Hello Dad.'

'Suzie. Nice to hear your voice, love. How's things?'

'We're all fine. Max finished painting this morning. It's looking lovely. The cot's arrived too. It's beautiful. Thank you so much for that, Dad.'

Arthur's mind travels back down the years. They had a second-hand cot ready and waiting for Suzie, and of course Dorothy had done so much sewing before the baby arrived, Arthur said she could open a shop.

'Are you excited?' he asks.

There is a slight pause before Suzie answers.

'Yes. I'm...'

'Nervous?'

Another pause.

'I'm frightened, Dad.'

'It's a big first.'

Arthur imagines Suzie biting her lip. She always does that when something worries her.

'I wish your mother was here for you.'

'Are you all right, Dad?'

Arthur feels his chest stiffen. What is the point of telling his daughter that he isn't all right, that he hasn't been all right since Dorothy died; that he probably won't be all right ever again. A sudden burst of laughter travels over the fence, gushes through the conservatory windows, rolls round the room like a paint-box spilling all its colours.

'It's the Indians next door,' he says, 'They're at it again.'

Suzie laughs. 'You mean they're enjoying themselves.'

Arthur sighs. Suzie's a lot like Dorothy. Always looking for the positive.

'You must come and stay, Dad, as soon as the baby's born.'

The last of next door's colour fades with the evening light. The wind is getting up as Arthur wanders into the garden. He and Dorothy used to share the work out here. He grew vegetables, cut the lawn. Dorothy saw to the flowers. He misses those in the house now, great vases of daffodils in spring, then on to snapdragons, roses, and Canterbury bells in summer, and later, Michaelmas daisies.

Dorothy was fond of simple things, thinks Arthur. How he'd ever ended up with such a wise and loving woman was beyond him. He'd seen himself as rather quiet, and dull. She said he was fun to be with.

Arthur knew he'd been a disappointment to his parents. By the time he went to university, he'd been convinced that he was probably the plainest, most boring individual this side of ancient Greece. Perhaps that was why he loved fossils so much. They were dead. They offered no criticism. They were all has-beens.

'Palaeontology, for heaven's sake!' his father had exclaimed. 'Whatever do you want to do that for? Fossils won't get you much of a job, you know.'

Arthur had blushed at this evidence of his failure yet again. But he'd stuck to his guns. And palaeontology it was. He found to his joy that he had an extraordinary ability in his chosen subject, a natural talent, as well as a keenness for digs.

'Scraping about in the dirt,' his mother called it.

He remembers telling Dorothy about his job when he first met her. By then he was a minor researcher and part-time university lecturer. He tried to make it sound not too bad. Dorothy's eyes had opened in wonder. What an exciting thing to be doing. Much more rewarding than teaching teenagers about Keats and Shakespeare, trying to share her own enthusiasm for literature. Especially when most of them would rather be listening to the latest groups, or going out with friends.

Dorothy.

The leaves are rustling now; twigs clank together; branches shake on the old apple tree. Lightning forks the sky; thunder rumbles in the distance.

The storm's one of the worst the neighbourhood's ever witnessed. It's as if the bedroom is lit by searchlight for a second, then darkness reasserts itself. Time and time again. The crash comes at around three in the morning. There's no electricity. Arthur goes downstairs on autopilot, fetches the torch from the kitchen, shines it round the room. The conservatory's a mess. Glass everywhere. The old apple tree has given up its branch to the fierce wind. It's crashed through the conservatory roof, and lies on the floor.

There is nothing to be done till morning.

Arthur's poring over the yellow pages when the doorbell goes. It's the Indian with the chocolate-coloured laugh. Arthur assumes he's come round to apologise for the racket yesterday. This is all I need right now, he thinks.

The Indian holds out his hand, introduces himself as Bijay.

'We've seen from our upstairs window,' he says, 'your sun lounge roof. May I offer you some assistance please?'

Arthur leads the way.

'We can do this between us in no time,' says Bijay. 'I will ask my good friend Jay to come and help us. I will go and fetch the necessary.'

Arthur stands for a minute looking at the mess. Then he rings Suzie. Max answers the phone, commiserates, and talks about the repairs.

'You should have that apple tree taken down,' he says.

'Dorothy loved that tree.'

'Look at it this way, Arthur. It's a danger to your house. It's leaning more and more. If you ask me, another branch'll come down in the next storm.'

Arthur changes the subject, asks after Suzie. Half his mind is elsewhere.

Everything has been exactly the same since Dorothy had died. Somehow it seems to lessen the distance between them.

Arthur puts the phone down with a sigh. Changes. They come and go before anyone can stop them. Now their first grandchild is on the way. If only Dorothy could be here. Arthur imagines the gentle voice of his late wife, and he weeps once more.

He's been sad for so long. Bordering on depression, the doctor said. Sent him to a woman from Cruise, who wanted to help. But Arthur was back to feeling unworthy of love, unworthy of friendship, sunk in the depths of gloom.

He hears the doorbell ringing again. It's the Indian, Bijay, and his friend. They've brought brushes and leather gloves. Arthur is anticipating their colourful laughter, echoing round his house all the morning, but they are quietly respectful. All three men work together as a team. At eleven o'clock Arthur makes them coffee. Bijay is interested in the photographs of Dorothy, of Suzie and Max. Later he asks Arthur if he would like to have lunch next door. His wife is expecting them.

Arthur hesitates. He hasn't been anywhere much for a couple of years.

'We would very much like you to join us,' says Bijay.

When Arthur meets Bijay's wife, she gives her blue glass laugh, and Arthur smiles. I'd know you anywhere, he thinks. She speaks gently to her three children, and shakes her head when Arthur says he thought they had more.

'We have many friends and relatives,' she says. She asks Arthur about his family. Her gentle questions about Dorothy encourage him to talk about her.

'I wish we had known her,' says Bijay's wife. 'You are a lucky man. You have her memory to cherish for the rest of your life, no matter what else comes your way.'

Arthur repeats these words as he stands in his damaged conservatory once more. A lucky man. If it hadn't been for last night, he'd never have got to know the Indian family next door. And how kind of them to ask him round again, for their barbeque next Saturday evening. He is actually looking forward to joining in their rainbow laughter.

That apple branch has done him a favour. You could call it a lucky break, he thinks.

Arthur stands there in his slippers, looking into the future with something that feels strangely like hope.

ABOUT THE STORIES

FEEDING THE BIRDS won 1st prize in the 2011 *Hampshire Chronicle* short story competition. It was published in the *Winchester Writers' Conference Anthology*.

THE NEXT INSTALMENT won 3rd prize in the 2011 Association of Christian Writers short story competition and was published on the ACW website.

THE WHOLE-FACE SMILE won 3rd prize in the 2016 Swanwick Writers Summer School short story competition. It has not been published before.

THE SIGN won 1st prize in the 2011 Speakeasy open creative writing competition, and was published on the Speakeasy website.

STARGAZING won 1st prize in the 2011 Writers Reign short story competition. It was published on the Writers Reign website.

A BIT OF PEACE AND QUIET won 2nd prize in the 2013 *Writers' News* competition. It was published online. www.writers-online.co.uk

MR WACKER'S BRIDGE won 3rd prize in the 2015 Chudleigh Phoenix short story competition, and was published online.

THE LAST RAYS won 3rd prize in the 2013 mags4dorset creative writing awards. It was published in *Town and Village Magazine*, April 2014.

RAINBOW LAUGHTER won 3rd prize in the 2011 New Eastbourne Writers short story competition. It was published online.

ABOUT THE AUTHOR

Veronica Bright is a prize-winning author of short fiction and drama. In 2005 she won the *Woman and Home* short story competition, and since then her works have won prizes in over forty competitions. They have also appeared online and in numerous anthologies. *Rainbow Laughter* is her third collection of stories.

Veronica and her family came to live in Cornwall in 1988, and she now claims to be Cornish by adoption. For many years she taught the reception class in a village primary school. She misses her own children now they've grown up and left home, but appreciates having time to write. Interruptions are welcomed if accompanied by tea and chocolate biscuits.

Veronica Bright is represented by Kiran Kataria of the Keane Kataria Literary Agency. Her monthly blog for aspiring writers may be found on her website. www.veronicabright.co.uk

Made in the USA
Columbia, SC
26 July 2017